# Hattie

## the Homeless Puppy

*Jenny Dale's Puppy Tales™ series*

# Hattie

## the Homeless Puppy

by Jenny Dale

Illustrated by Susan Hellard

A Working Partners Book

MACMILLAN CHILDREN'S BOOKS

*Special thanks to Narinder Dhami*

First published 2000 by Macmillan Children's Books

This edition published 2015 by Macmillan Children's Books
an imprint of Pan Macmillan
20 New Wharf Road, London N1 9RR
Associated companies throughout the world
www.panmacmillan.com

Created by Working Partners Limited

ISBN 978-1-4472-9960-8

1 3 5 7 9 8 6 4 2

A CIP catalogue record for this book is available from the British Library.

Printed and bound by CPI Group (UK) Ltd, Croydon CR0 4YY

# Chapter One

"Mummy! Look at that cute little puppy!"

Hattie's ears pricked up. She was sitting gloomily on the beach, wondering if she was going to get any breakfast that day. If only she was still at home with Alice, she thought miserably. Then she would be tucking into a big bowl of *K9 Meaty Chunks* right at this very minute.

"Oh, Mummy, I think she's hungry," said the little girl anxiously. "Can I give her some of the crisps we brought for later?"

Hattie barked, "Yes please!" and wagged her tail. She loved crisps, especially cheese and onion flavour.

"Well, I don't know, Janie." The girl's mother frowned and looked up and down the beach. It was still quite early, so there weren't many people around. "The puppy's owner might not like it."

"I don't know where my owner is!" Hattie barked sadly. "Please give me

some crisps – I'm hungry!"

"But I think the puppy's here on its own," Janie said, looking upset. "It must be lost. Or maybe it's a stray and no one wants it!"

Janie's mum looked down at the sweet white puppy. "Oh, I can't believe that. She's such a lovely little dog, and she looks as if she's been well looked after. Maybe the owner lives nearby and has just let her out for a while."

"They shouldn't do that," Janie said, sounding annoyed. "She hasn't got a collar on, and anyway, the poor thing might get run over." She bent down and held her hand out to Hattie.

Hattie crept forward and sniffed the girl's fingers, her tail still wagging. Mmm! She could smell lovely breakfast smells like buttered toast and scrambled eggs. Alice sometimes shared a bit of her breakfast with Hattie, and scrambled eggs had been one of their favourites.

Hattie's stomach gurgled, and she

whined, pressing her little body against Janie's legs.

"Oh, Mummy, *please* can I give her some of my crisps?" Janie pleaded.

Her mother gave in. "Oh, all right. But don't put them down on the sand. Here, put them on my newspaper."

Janie spread the newspaper out and poured some crisps on to it.

Hattie pounced on them eagerly. They weren't cheese and onion, but they tasted delicious. She licked up every last scrap and then whined for more.

"She's *very* hungry, Mummy," Janie said, giving Hattie the rest of the crisps. "She *must* be a stray," she said as they watched the puppy gobble them up.

Her mother nodded. "If she's still here tomorrow, we'll call the RSPCA. The poor thing's very young to be out here on her own. Still, at least it looks like it's going to be another warm day." The sky was very blue, and, although it was early, the sun was already quite warm. "Come on, Janie, we must go."

"Bye, little puppy." Janie walked away reluctantly, giving Hattie a wave. "I'll bring you some biscuits tomorrow!"

"Thanks, I like *K9 Crunch* best!" Hattie barked hopefully, wagging her tail. She liked Janie. She was very kind, just like Alice . . .

Hattie whined softly. Two days ago, when she belonged to Alice, she had been the happiest little puppy and her life had been cosy and safe. Now she was all alone.

Hattie slumped down on to the sand, put her nose between her paws and closed her eyes. She thought back to when she had gone to live with Alice and her family.

At first, Hattie had been quite scared of leaving her mum, and Alice's three-year-old brother, Michael, had seemed very rough and noisy. But Alice and her mum and dad, Mr and Mrs Thomas, had been kind and gentle. And they showed Michael how to be gentle too.

Hattie had soon grown to love Alice and her family – even Michael. But she loved Alice best of all.

"Oh, Alice," Hattie whined, "I wish I could see you again!"

"Hattie! Hattie!"

Hattie opened her eyes. A spotted Dalmatian was loping across the wet sand towards her, barking her name.

"Hello, Mollie," Hattie barked back. Hattie had been living on the beach for two days now. She had made friends with some of the dogs whose owners brought them there for a walk.

"How are you, Hattie?" Mollie bounded up to her. "Where did you sleep last night?"

"In one of the caves," Hattie said bravely, trying not to think about her usual sleeping place, which was snuggled up next to Alice. "At least it was warm and dry."

"Come with me," Mollie barked, dancing playfully round the puppy and kicking up showers of sand. "My owner's got lots of dog biscuits in his pocket!"

"I've had some crisps for breakfast," Hattie said. "But I'd love some biscuits!" She raced across the sand after Mollie towards a young man in jeans and a sweatshirt.

"Kevin! Kevin!" Mollie romped around her owner, nipping at his shins affectionately. "Hattie wants a biscuit!"

"Hi, pup," Mollie's owner said. He squatted down to pat Hattie. Then he felt in his pocket for a biscuit and handed it to her.

Hattie wolfed it down eagerly and then looked up, hoping for more.

"You know, I'm getting a bit worried about this little pup, Mollie," Kevin said, as Hattie munched her fourth biscuit. "This is the third day she's been here on her own."

But for a short while, Hattie forgot her troubles. She and Mollie raced down to the sea together and played in the waves, having a great time.

"This is fun!" Mollie barked as they splashed around.

"Can we play too?" A Cairn terrier was running towards them as fast as her short legs could carry her. She was trying – but failing – to keep up with a long-legged grey mongrel.

"Hello, Bonnie, hello, Rex," Hattie woofed. Bonnie and Rex were also two of her new friends. They shared the same owner, Mrs Malone, a kind-faced old lady who had given Hattie a bit of her egg sandwich the day before.

"Our owner's got a bone for you," Bonnie panted as she skidded to a halt on the wet sand.

"Yum!" Hattie was pleased. She could bury that and keep it for her dinner later on.

"Come on, let's play!" Rex barked, jumping right into the middle of a large wave.

Hattie joined in. She enjoyed herself enormously – until she suddenly noticed something. A little girl like Alice, wearing a red swimsuit, was playing on the beach with her puppy. She was throwing a ball into the shallows, and the puppy was rushing in to fetch it.

The girl was squealing with delight and the puppy was barking, and they were both having a wonderful time.

That's just what Alice and I were doing a few days ago, Hattie thought, and she felt miserable all over again.

"What's the matter, Hattie?" Bonnie yapped. "Are you thinking about your owner?"

Hattie looked even sadder. "Yes," she yapped back. "I really miss her."

"You still haven't told us why you're homeless now," Mollie woofed. "How did it happen?"

Hattie didn't really want to talk about what had happened to her because it

made her feel so unhappy. But Mollie, Bonnie and Rex were her friends, so she decided to tell them.

Hattie looked at them with sad brown eyes. "I'll tell you exactly what happened," she woofed. "It all started two days ago when I was on holiday with Alice and her family . . ."

# Chapter Two

"Hattie, are you all right in there?"

Hattie's tail began to wag madly as she heard Alice's voice outside the door of the camper van. Hattie had been stuck in her car kennel for what seemed like ages, while Mrs Thomas had driven them along the coastal road. Although Hattie had plenty of room and her favourite blanket and toys, she was longing for a good run-around outside. She was so glad that the van had stopped at last!

"Hello, girl!" Alice slid back the door and came into the van. Mrs Thomas and Mr Thomas followed, carrying Michael.

"Not much longer now, and then we'll be at the campsite where we're staying tonight," said Mrs Thomas.

Hattie barked happily and licked Alice's fingers as she pushed them through the wire mesh of the car kennel.

At first the puppy had thought it was very strange when Alice had told her

18

that they were going away on their "holidays". Hattie couldn't understand why anyone would want to get into a tiny home on wheels when they had a much bigger house to live in!

But if "holidays" meant being with Alice all the time and travelling around to all sorts of new exciting places with all sorts of interesting new smells, Hattie was all for it!

The only thing she wasn't too keen on at first was that she had to travel in her car kennel in the back of the van. Alice and the rest of the family sat in the cabin at the front. But Hattie had got used to the kennel, and she knew it kept her safe.

"Hello, Hattie!" Michael was already struggling to get out of his dad's arms so that he could get to the puppy. "Want Hattie!"

"No, Michael, Hattie's not coming out yet," his dad said firmly. Then he turned to Alice. "We'll have something to eat first at the mobile café. Then you can take Hattie for a good walk before we set off again."

"Can I borrow that handkerchief of yours again, Dad?" Alice asked, grinning. "Like this morning, remember?"

Just before they set off on their holiday, Mr Thomas had decided that Hattie's tiny puppy collar was now too tight for her. But Hattie needed to go for a walk, so Mr Thomas had made a collar for her out of a knotted handkerchief, and Alice had tied Hattie's lead round it. Everyone had thought she looked very funny.

"We mustn't forget to buy a proper new collar at the next town we visit," Mrs Thomas said, smiling as she took a struggling Michael out of the camper van. Mr Thomas followed her to the mobile café.

"I'll take you for a walk soon, Hattie," Alice said.

The puppy began to whine. "Can't you take me now?"

"Sorry, Hattie." Alice pushed some dog biscuits through the wire mesh, and then checked to make sure the puppy had some water. "I won't be long, I promise." She stroked the tip of Hattie's nose, and Hattie wagged her tail happily.

"Alice?" Mr Thomas peered into the van. "Make sure you leave the door open a little so that Hattie gets some fresh air. It's very hot today, and it should be safe enough with us so near."

"Yes, I will," Alice said, as she left to go and choose her lunch.

Lots of cars and caravans and other camper vans were parked near the Thomases' van. Through the slightly open door Hattie could also see people outside, sitting at wooden picnic benches or standing in a queue next to the mobile café.

A cool sea breeze wafted in, bringing

with it some very interesting smells!
Hattie raised her head and sniffed.
She could smell something very tasty
indeed: bacon – one of her favourites!
Maybe Alice would save her a bit.

Hattie crunched up her biscuits, had
a long drink of water and then sat down

patiently to wait for Alice. But someone else came instead.

"Hattie?" Michael peered into the van, a big beam on his face. "Hello, Hattie!"

Hattie barked, "Hello, Michael!" back. She watched as the toddler heaved himself into the van, puffing and panting with the effort, and then came over to her cage.

"Want lunch, Hattie?" Michael asked the puppy with a big smile. "Good dog!"

Hattie looked hopefully at Michael, but he didn't seem to have anything for her to eat. Instead, he began fiddling with the catch on the car kennel door.

"Oh, are you going to let me out?" Hattie yapped, although she didn't think he would. Michael had often tried to undo the catch, but he'd never managed to do it.

"Come on, Hattie, good dog!" Michael's round face was pink with effort as he wrestled with the catch. "Walk!"

"OK!" Hattie barked. "But I'll just check out the bacon smells first, if that's all right with you!"

A few moments later the door swung open, and Michael squealed proudly. "Come on, Hattie! Walk!"

Hattie shot out quickly. She gave

Michael a quick lick before rushing out of the van. The delicious smell of bacon was even stronger outside! She looked around eagerly and saw Alice and her mum and dad at one of the nearby picnic benches.

She was just about to dash over to them when she noticed a man standing outside the mobile café. He was taking a bite out of a huge sandwich. As he did so, a large piece of bacon shot out and landed on the grass. The man didn't notice as he hurried back to his car.

Hattie's mouth watered. Mmm! she thought. I won't let *that* go to waste!

The puppy rushed over to gulp down

the bit of bacon. Neither Alice nor
her parents, who were busy sorting
out the food and drink they'd bought,
noticed her.

"Hattie!" Michael called. "Hattie!"
"Where on earth is Michael?" Mrs
Thomas heard the toddler yelling and

beckoned to him. "Michael, I told you not to wander off! Come and have something to eat."

"Hattie go walk!" Michael said, toddling over to his mother.

"Yes, Michael, we'll take Hattie for a walk after we've eaten," Alice said, waving her sandwich at him.

Michael noticed the food for the first time and beamed, forgetting all about Hattie. "Michael want hamburger!" he said.

"No, I've got you a sandwich," said Mrs Thomas.

"ME WANT HAMBURGER!" Michael roared furiously.

Meanwhile, Hattie was just about to trot over and join the family when she noticed another interesting smell. She followed her nose, which led her round to the back of the mobile café.

There were bags of rubbish there and lots of titbits on the ground. Hattie found some more bacon, half a sausage and a grilled tomato, although she wasn't quite so keen on that. She was just hoovering up half a buttered scone when she heard a very familiar noise.

It was the sound of the family's camper van starting up! Hattie froze. Oh no! Were Alice and the rest of the family going to drive off and leave her behind?

# Chapter Three

Panting from fright, Hattie raced back over to the row of parked vehicles. She spotted the blue and white camper van and charged towards it, her heart pounding. Why were they going without her? Alice had never left her behind before!

Hattie scrambled through the open

door of the van and flopped down on the floor. She was safe!

Or was she?

Hattie sniffed the air. It smelled different. And where was her car kennel with her blanket and toys and water bowl?

Just then, Hattie heard a strange woman's voice. She was in the driving seat in the front cabin. "Steve, did you shut the van door?" That wasn't Mrs Thomas!

"OK, I'll do it now," the person called Steve said grumpily. He climbed out and slammed the door shut on Hattie.

Hattie whimpered. She felt *very*

frightened. She wasn't in her family's camper van at all. She'd jumped into someone else's van! Hattie could hardly believe what she'd done. How could she have been so stupid?

"One of these days we'll drive off and you'll have left that door wide open!" the woman said crossly. "You're always forgetting to close it!"

Hattie knew she somehow had to tell the strangers that she was locked in their camper van by mistake. She tried to bark. But she was so frightened that she could only manage a squeak.

Just at that moment, the woman revved up the engine again, drowning the sound of Hattie's squeak. Then the van pulled away noisily, gathering speed all the time.

At last Hattie managed to bark. "Stop! Please stop!" she howled at the top of her voice. "There's been a terrible mistake!"

Desperately, Hattie kept barking – but no one seemed to hear her. Her panic grew with every mile the van travelled. Where were these people taking her? Would they take her back to Alice? Hattie could hardly bear to think what might happen to her if they didn't.

At last, the van began to slow down. Hattie stopped barking to see

what would happen next.

As the noise of the engine died away, Hattie could hear the man and woman arguing in the front cabin.

"I'm telling you, I heard a dog barking!" the woman insisted. "I'm sure it's in the back of our van!"

"Don't be daft, Suzie!" Steve said

crossly. "How can there be a dog in the back? We haven't *got* a dog!"

"I *heard* it!" Suzie snapped.

Hattie heard the two cabin doors open. Both of the people in front were climbing out.

"It probably jumped in because you left the side door open, Stupid!" Suzie snapped again.

Hattie thought Steve and Suzie didn't sound very nice at all. She crept underneath the table and waited, trembling.

"Just a minute, Steve," Suzie said in a worried voice. "What if it's a *big* dog like a Dobermann or a German Shepherd?"

"I've told you, there's no dog in there!"

Steve said. But now he didn't sound too sure. "Get me that big spanner from the toolbox," he added. "Just in case."

Hattie wondered what a spanner was. Maybe it was some kind of doggy treat. Maybe these people weren't so bad after all. Wide-eyed, she watched as the door opened slowly, and Steve and Suzie looked in. They didn't look too frightening.

"Is . . . is anyone there?" Steve asked in a trembling voice.

Hattie gave a bark and shot out from under the table. "Yes, me! Please take me back to Alice!" she woofed.

Startled, Suzie screamed and Steve

leaped back, dropping the spanner with a clatter.

Scared out of her wits, Hattie ran for the door, jumped out and fled.

There were some steps at the side of the road that led to a wide, sandy beach. Hattie ran down them and kept running until she felt safe.

# Chapter Four

"And that's how I came to be homeless and living on this beach," Hattie barked sadly. She looked round at Mollie, Bonnie and Rex. "Now I don't know if I'll ever see Alice again."

"That's terrible," Bonnie yapped, shaking her shaggy head in sympathy. "What a shame."

"I was homeless too until Mrs Malone took me in," Rex snuffled. "It's a hard life."

Hattie whined in agreement.

Mollie barked suddenly. "I've had a great idea! Why don't you look for a new owner, Hattie?"

"I don't want a new owner," Hattie woofed unhappily. "No one could be better than Alice!"

"But any owner is better than being homeless," Rex pointed out wisely. "As long as they're kind to you."

Hattie thought about that. As she looked down the beach she saw that the girl in the red swimsuit was still playing happily with her puppy. Maybe she *could* find someone else who would love her . . .

"All right," she barked, "but how do I find a new owner?"

"Well, people like dogs who are friendly," Mollie woofed, confidently. "They like you to jump up at them and lick them and bark very loudly!"

"Do they?" Hattie barked back, impressed. Alice's mum had always told her off when she'd made too much noise at home!

Bonnie and Rex didn't look quite so sure, either. But just then, their owner, Mrs Malone, came over to them, carrying their leads.

"Oh, here's your little friend again," Mrs Malone said, fishing in her pocket. "I've brought you a bone." And she bent down to pat Hattie.

Hattie took the bone. "Thank you. Maybe you could be my new owner," she woofed hopefully.

"It would be great," Bonnie yapped.

"But we live in a very small flat, and I heard Mrs Malone say she can't have any more pets."

Hattie slumped down on the sand, disappointed.

"Mrs Malone! How are you today?"

They all looked round. An elderly lady with white hair was making her way across the beach towards them.

"That's Mrs O'Brien," Bonnie told Hattie. "She's a friend of my owner."

"Maybe *she's* looking for a puppy!" Hattie barked eagerly.

"Remember what I said," Mollie reminded her. "Be friendly!"

"Oh, hello, Mrs O'Brien." Mrs Malone

waved at her. "Did you come to see that stray puppy I was telling you about?"

"Yes, I did," Mrs O'Brien called back. At that moment she caught sight of Hattie. "Well, isn't she adorable? Who on earth would abandon such a beautiful little pup?"

She didn't have time to say any more. Hattie flew across the sand towards her, barking as loudly as she could. She flung herself at Mrs O'Brien's legs, jumping up at her. "Yes, I am adorable – and I'm really friendly, too!" Hattie barked. "*Please* take me home with you!"

"Eek!" Mrs O'Brien, who wasn't very steady on her feet anyway, began to

44

teeter backwards. Mrs Malone had to rush over, pick Hattie up and take her out of the way.

"Oh dear," Mrs O'Brien said, looking rather pale. "This pup's rather too lively for me. Maybe an older dog would suit me better."

"Yes, I think it would," Mrs Malone agreed with a sigh. She put Hattie back down on the sand.

"No, it wouldn't!" Hattie whined. She sat on the sand watching miserably as Mrs O'Brien said her goodbyes and walked off as quickly as she could. Mrs O'Brien didn't want her, Hattie thought sadly. Would *anyone* give her a home?

# Chapter Five

"Well, *that* didn't work, did it?" Hattie barked sadly to the others as they followed Mrs Malone down the beach.

"Sorry, Hattie," Mollie woofed. "It was all my fault. I thought people liked friendly dogs!"

"Yes, but not all of us are as lively as you Dalmatians!" Bonnie yapped.

"Some people like quiet dogs who aren't any trouble," Rex added.

Hattie thought about that. It was true that Mr and Mrs Thomas were always pleased with her when she was behaving herself and not chewing things or barking too much. The trouble was, Hattie sometimes enjoyed chewing things and barking her head off! But if getting a new home meant being quiet all the time, she would have to do it.

"Look, there's that boy again." Bonnie barked. A boy of about seven was coming along the beach, carrying his bucket and spade, while his mum followed with a baby in a buggy. "His name's Andy, and he loves dogs – he always stops and pats us," Bonnie told Hattie.

"I've heard him asking his mum if he can have a puppy too," Rex added.

"Maybe I can go home with him then!" Hattie said excitedly.

"Yes, but don't knock him over when you say hello!" Bonnie warned her.

"Oh, look, Mum! A puppy!" Andy

cried, spotting Hattie.

Hattie's heart thumped with excitement. She had to try her hardest to be quiet and sensible. She mustn't frighten Andy away!

Andy ran over to Hattie and ruffled the soft white fur on her ears. "Do you want to play with me?" he asked.

Hattie stayed where she was, even though she was longing to jump up at the little boy.

"Come on," Andy urged Hattie, looking rather disappointed. "Come and help me build a huge sandcastle."

Hattie stood up and trotted quietly across the beach with Andy. She didn't bark or run or do anything noisy or lively.

When Andy started to dig, she sat down and watched him. Even when he stopped digging to stroke her, she didn't lick his hand or jump up at him.

"You're very quiet for a puppy," Andy said, as he stuck a flag in the top of his sandcastle. "My friend Matt has got a puppy called Sam, and Sam's not quiet at all!"

"Andy!" The boy's mother was calling him from higher up the beach where she was sitting with the baby.

"Coming!" Andy called back. He scrambled to his feet and ran off, forgetting all about Hattie.

"What about me?" Hattie whined sadly, longing to get up and charge after him.

Mollie, Rex and Bonnie hurried over to her.

"That didn't work either," Hattie said glumly. "Andy didn't want a *quiet* puppy!"

"Never mind," Bonnie yapped. "You'll soon find someone else."

"Alice loved me when I was noisy *and* when I was quiet," Hattie snuffled miserably.

"Mollie!" Kevin was coming towards the Dalmatian. "Time to go."

"Bonnie! Rex!" Mrs Malone whistled to her two dogs from further down the beach. "Let's go home now."

"See you later, Hattie," Mollie barked.

"And don't worry," Rex woofed kindly, "I'm sure you'll find a new home very soon."

But deep down, Hattie didn't *want* a new home. She already had the best home for her, with the best owner – Alice! If only she could hear Alice calling her to go home, Hattie thought sadly.

She watched Steve and Mrs Malone clip leads on to their dogs' collars. If only Alice was here right now . . .

*"Hattie!"*

# Chapter Six

Hattie thought she must have imagined the voice calling her name. it sounded like Alice – but it couldn't be.

"Hattie! Oh, Hattie, I've found you at last!"

There was that voice again. Hattie stared around the beach, her heart beating fast. Kevin, Mrs Malone and their dogs were all looking round too.

A fair-haired girl was racing across the sand towards them, a huge smile on her face. Hattie began to tremble all over with joy. It really *was* Alice!

Hattie didn't wait another second. She tore across the beach as fast as her short legs could carry her. "Alice!" she barked. "It really is you!"

Alice scooped the puppy up in her arms and hugged her hard. "Oh, Hattie!" she cried, burying her face in Hattie's soft white coat. "I thought I'd lost you for ever. We've been looking *everywhere*!"

Hattie licked every bit of Alice's neck and face that she could reach. "I'm so glad you found me, Alice," she barked happily. "I've really, really missed you!"

Mollie, Rex and Bonnie were jumping around their owners in delight. Kevin and Mrs Malone looked on, smiling.

"Oh, Hattie, thank goodness you're safe!" Mrs Thomas said as she rushed over with Mr Thomas, who was carrying

Michael. "We've all been so worried!"

"I think everyone on the beach has been worrying about this little pup too!" Kevin said.

"Yes, some of us have been feeding her," Mrs Malone smiled. "I was going to ring the RSPCA if Hattie was still here tomorrow."

Kevin nodded. "So was I."

"Oh, thank you *very* much for looking after her," Alice said. She was clinging onto Hattie as if she was afraid that the puppy would disappear again.

"How did you lose her?" Kevin asked.

Mr Thomas glanced at Michael, who was leaning over to pet Hattie. "Well, we think this little terror let Hattie out of her car kennel in the back of our camper van when we stopped for something to eat. We looked around for her, but no luck."

Mrs Thomas then took up the tale. "We didn't bother to come here to search because this town is miles from where we lost Hattie. We didn't think a little pup like her could travel this far on her own. But then something very strange happened . . ."

"Yes," Alice said, "we were asking around the campsite where we were staying for the last night of our holiday, and we saw a camper van that looked exactly the same as ours . . ."

Hattie was listening to the story with interest. When she heard that, her ears pricked up. Alice's family must have met Steve and Suzie!

"The people who owned it told us that they'd found a dog in the back," Alice went on. "And it had run off on to the beach when they'd reached this town. So we came here straight away." Alice hugged Hattie again. "And now the first thing we're going to do is buy you a new collar and name tag!"

"Good!" Hattie barked, smothering her owner in kisses.

"'Bye, Hattie," Mollie called as Kevin

led her away. "I'm glad you found Alice again!"

"'Bye, Hattie," Bonnie and Rex added too.

Hattie was sad to say goodbye to her friends, but she was so pleased to be going home with Alice. What if Alice hadn't found her? Hattie shivered and decided not to think about it.

As Alice carried Hattie back to the

camper van, she whispered in Hattie's ear. "Mum says we're going to take you to the vet when we get home."

Hattie looked at Alice, puzzled. "Why? I'm not ill," she yapped.

"The vet will give you a microchip," Alice went on. "So I'll always be able to find you."

Hattie wagged her tail and gave Alice a quick lick. She didn't know what a *micro-chip* was, but she loved chips – especially with a nice bit of fish. And if having a chip meant that Hattie would always be with Alice, that was even better!

Hattie didn't want to be homeless ever again.